The Hums of Pooh

Lyrics by
POOH

Introduction and Notes by
A. A. MILNE

Decorations by
E. H. SHEPARD

Additional Lyric by
EEYORE

Methuen Children's Books
LONDON

Original edition of THE HUMS OF POOH
first published 1929

This selection © *1972 by Spenser Curtis Brown,*
Executor of the Estate of the late A. A. Milne
Reprinted four times
Reprinted 1983
by Methuen Children's Books Ltd
Magnet paperback edition
first published 1983
by Methuen Children's Books Ltd
11 New Fetter Lane,
London EC4P 4EE

Individual copyright for text and illustrations:
WINNIE-THE-POOH *copyright 1926*
THE HOUSE AT POOH CORNER *copyright 1928*
THE HUMS OF POOH *copyright 1929*
All rights reserved
Printed in Great Britain by
Blantyre Printing and Binding Ltd,
Glasgow

ISBN 0 416 67210 8 (hardback)
ISBN 0 416 42910 6 (paperback)

Publisher's Note

The publishers would like to point out that the original edition of *The Hums of Pooh*, published in 1929, included music by H. Fraser-Simson. Although this pocket-sized edition does not contain the music, references to musical points will be found in the Introduction and in some of A. A. Milne's notes on the Hums as these have been reprinted without any alteration. Six of the Hums included in this book now re-appear in *The Pooh Song Book,* a new collection of fifteen songs with piano accompaniment and simple guitar chords (these are marked with an asterisk on the Contents page).

The Hums themselves, again reprinted from the original edition, include musical effects, such as repeats, which are not found in *Winnie-the-Pooh* and *The House at Pooh Corner*.

A. A. Milne's 'stage directions' have also been retained and children may now hear and watch these songs, adapted for the theatre by Julian Slade, being performed in the musical play Winnie-the-Pooh at Christmas.

The original edition of *The Hums of Pooh* was dedicated to Cicely Fraser-Simson in the following verse:

As Pooh is inspired by a hum or a whistle he
 Hears in the tops of the Trees,
As Eeyore is moved by the crunch of the thistle he
 Pulls at his negligent ease,
So we were inspired by the humour which Cicely
 Brought to the singing of these.

Contents

Introduction

If you have read (and I don't know why you should, but it will make it very awkward for me if you haven't) two books called *Winnie-the-Pooh* and *The House at Pooh Corner*, then you will need no introduction to this one. For when you see it, you will say (at least, I hope you will) 'Ah, here it is at last!' And here it is.

But if you haven't read these other two books, then, as I say, you have made it very awkward for me. Because what I want to say, and keep on saying, is 'What! You *haven't*? Well! What *have* you been doing all this time?'—and I oughtn't to say this, because (you may as well know; it's bound to come out) I am the author of those two books. I was taught in the nursery (perhaps wrongly) that 'Self-praise is no recommendation'—(one 'c' and two 'm's.' Some people do it the other way)—but sometimes I think that if one doesn't praise oneself, and there's nobody else noticing, who *is* going to do it? When I write an Introduction for somebody else's book, I never let go the pen until all my readers are trooping off to the bookshops, and saying 'I want two copies of all the books which this man, I've forgotten his name, has written,' but the bother is that I can never get anybody else to write an Introduction to *my* books. They say 'Oh, no, you can do it much better yourself'; and I daresay I can; but I can't Let Myself Go as they could. I did say to Mr. Fraser-Simson, 'Suppose we have two Introductions, and *I'll* tell everybody how good the music is, and *you* tell everybody how good the words are, and then nobody can possibly say we are being conceited,' but he wouldn't. He says he can't write. I suppose he puts two 'c's' and one 'm'—a pity.

Very well, then, I've got to do it myself, and this is what I've got to explain. In those two books which you haven't read . . . WHICH YOU HAVEN'T READ . . . no, no, let us hush it up—which you haven't read—there was a bear called Pooh, who lived in the Forest, and hummed as he went about his way. If you had read the books (I am sorry, but I must say it again) you would know all about these hums of his, and just what part of each book each one came in, and what Pooh was doing at the time, and who Tigger and

Eeyore and Christopher Robin were. And as you looked through this book, recognizing old friends, you would say of each one, 'I've often wondered what the tune of *this* was, and now I know.' But, as it is, you will be saying, 'Rumty Tiddle-y tiddle-y tum, rum tiddle-y tum tum—oh, no it's B *flat*—tum *tum*. A very pretty tune, but what's it all *about*?' So at the beginning of each song, I have explained, as quickly as possible, what it *is* all about.

And, turning back to those sensible people, those dear friends, those adventurers, who *have* read the books and know them by heart, perhaps it would be as well if you too, when you sing these songs in public, were first to read aloud these little explanations. For you never know. People are funny; and the old gentleman with whiskers in the middle of the third row *may* take the Pooh books to bed with him every night . . . or he *may* have thought that this was a meeting of the Royal Asiatic Society. So, if the policeman mis-directed him at the corner, or he thought it was Tuesday, you can spare him something of the surprise by not sailing into the song until you have given him these few words of warning.

And, finally, to those same dear friends, (since this may be the last time that the word 'Pooh' will leave my nib) may I say, 'Thank you for having loved him.' He will be very proud if you sing his songs, and so keep him for ever in your memory.

A. A. MILNE

Isn't it Funny . . .

One day when Pooh was out walking, he came to a very tall tree, and from the top of the tree there came a loud buzzing noise. Well, Pooh knew what that meant—honey; so he began to climb the tree. And as he climbed, he sang a little song to himself. Really it was two little songs, because he climbed twenty-seven feet nine-and-a-half inches in between the two verses. So if the second verse is higher than the first, you will know why.

Buzzily

Isn't it funny
How a bear likes honey?
Buzz! Buzz! Buzz!
I wonder why he does?

It's a very funny thought that, if Bears were
                                                    Bees,
They'd build their nests at the *bottom* of trees.
And that being so (if the Bees were Bears),
We shouldn't have to climb up all these stairs.

How Sweet to be a Cloud

When Pooh had fallen from the top of the honey-tree to the bottom (in the quickest time that anybody had ever done it in) he picked himself out of the gorse-bush, and tried to think of another way of getting to the honey. So he thought of floating up to the top of the tree on the end of a blue balloon, and trying to look like a Small Cloud in a very blue sky. And so as to deceive the bees entirely, he sang a small Cloud Song, such as a cloud might sing. Here it is . . . .

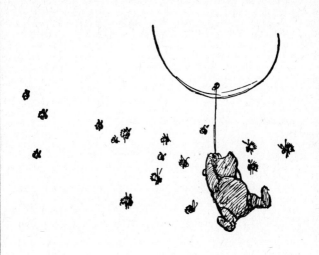

Floatingly

How sweet to be a Cloud
Floating in the Blue!
Ev'ry little cloud
Always sings aloud.

'How sweet to be a Cloud
Floating in the Blue!'
It makes him very proud
To be a little Cloud.
How sweet to be a Cloud
Floating in the Blue!

It's very very Funny . . .

One day Pooh and Piglet were trying to catch a Heffalump, and they decided that the best way was to dig a Heffalump Trap and put something in it which Heffalumps liked. And Piglet thought that what they liked best was Honey, because then Pooh would have to go back to his house and get some; and Pooh thought that they liked Haycorns best, because then Piglet would have to go back; but Piglet thought first. So Pooh went back and got his last pot of honey for the Trap. And in the night he woke up feeling very hungry, and went to his cupboard . . . and when he couldn't find any he sang this song.

Anxiously

It's very, very funny,
'Cos I *know* I had some honey;
'Cos it had a label on,
            saying HUNNY.

A goloptious full-up pot too,
And I don't know where it's got to,
No, I don't know where it's gone—
            Well, it's FUNNY.

Cottleston Pie

This is a song which you sing when anybody says anything which you don't quite understand. You could say 'What?' or 'I beg your pardon,' but Pooh always used to sing *Cottleston Pie*, which is a song he made up for singing when his brain felt fluffy.

Wonderingly

Cottleston, Cottleston, Cottleston Pie.
A fly can't bird, but a bird can fly.
Ask me a riddle and I reply:
'*Cottleston, Cottleston, Cottleston Pie.*'

Cottleston, Cottleston, Cottleston Pie.
A fish can't whistle and neither can I.
Ask me a riddle and I reply:
'*Cottleston, Cottleston, Cottleston Pie.*'

Cottleston, Cottleston, Cottleston Pie.
Why does a chicken, I don't know why.
Ask me a riddle and I reply:
'*Cottleston, Cottleston, Cottleston Pie.*'

Lines Written by a Bear of Very Little Brain

The title of this song is *Lines Written by a Bear of Very Little Brain*, and as that describes it, I won't say any more about it, except that Kanga said 'Yes it is, isn't it?' just as the fifth verse was beginning. So we shall never know what happened on Friday.

Briskly

On Monday, when the sun is hot
I wonder to myself a lot:
'Now is it true, or is it not,
That what is which and which is what?'

On Tuesday, when it hails and snows,
The feeling on me grows and grows
That hardly anybody knows
If those are these or these are those.

On Wednesday, when the sky is blue,
And I have nothing else to do,
I sometimes wonder if it's true
That who is what and what is who.

On Thursday, when it starts to freeze
And hoar-frost twinkles on the trees,
How very readily one sees
That these are whose—but whose are these?

On Friday—
On Friday—
On Friday—
'What did happen on Friday?' (*Spoken*)

Sing Ho! for the Life of a Bear!

This is a song sung by Pooh when he feels Ho-ish. Some people, when they feel like this, either look about for somebody to push over, or else they break something accidentally, but Pooh works it off by singing a small Ho-song.

With plenty of spirit

Sing Ho! for the life of a Bear!
Sing Ho! for the life of a Bear!
I don't much mind if it rains or snows,
'Cos I've got a lot of honey on my nice new
nose!
I don't much care if it snows or thaws,
'Cos I've got a lot of honey on my nice clean
paws!

Sing Ho! for the life of a Bear!
Sing Ho! for a Pooh!
And I'll have a little something in an hour or
two!

Sing Ho! for a Bear!
Sing Ho! for a Pooh!
And I'll have a little something in an hour or
two!

They all went off to discover the Pole

This is the song which Pooh sang on the Expotition to the North Pole, led by Christopher Robin. When he got to the end of the first verse Christopher Robin said 'Hush'! (because they were coming to a dangerous place) which explains why there isn't a second verse.

Expeditiously

They all went off to discover the Pole,
Owl and Piglet and Rabbit and all;
It's a Thing you Discover, as I've been tole
By Owl and Piglet and Rabbit and all.
Eeyore, Christopher Robin and Pooh
And Rabbit's relations all went too—
And where the Pole was none of them knew...
Sing Hey! for Owl and Rabbit and all!
Sing Hey! for Owl and Rabbit and all his
   friends and relations and Piglet and Pooh
                         and Kanga and Roo
And Eeyore and Christopher Robin and all!

3 Cheers for Pooh!

This is an Anxious Pooh Song. Pooh Bear was anxious, because Christopher Robin was giving a party to celebrate something which Pooh had done, and Pooh was afraid that perhaps none of the others at the party would know about his Brave Rescue of Piglet (which is what he had done), and say 'Why?' when Christopher Robin said 'Three Cheers for Pooh!' or whatever you say after a Brave Rescue. So he made up a song about how awkward it would be if everybody said 'Why?' and 'Who?' and 'I didn't hear.' This is the song.

Cheerily

3 Cheers for Pooh!
(*For Who?*)
For Pooh—
(*Why what did he do?*)
I thought you knew;
He saved his friend from a wetting!
3 Cheers for Bear!
(*For where?*)
For Bear—
He couldn't swim,
But he rescued him!

(*He rescued who?*)
Oh, listen, do!
I am talking of Pooh—
(*Of who?*)
Of Pooh!
(*I'm sorry I keep forgetting.*)
Well, Pooh was a Bear of Enormous Brain—
(*Just say it again!*)
Of enormous brain—
(*Of enormous what?*)
Well, he ate a lot,
And I don't know if he could swim or not,
But he managed to float on a sort of boat
(*On a sort of what?*)
Well, a sort of pot—
So now let's give him three hearty cheers
(*So now let's give him three hearty whiches?*)
And hope he'll be with us for years and years,
And grow in health and wisdom and riches!

3 cheers for Pooh!
(*For who?*)
For Pooh—
3 cheers for Bear!
(*For where?*)
For Bear—
3 cheers for the wonderful Winnie the Pooh!
(*Just tell me somebody—*
WHAT DID HE DO?)

The More it Snows . . .

This is Pooh's favourite song, and mine too. It is described in the catalogues as an 'Outdoor Hum for Snowy Weather' and there is a special footnote by Mr. Brown, the manager, to say that the chorus can be sung separately while doing stoutness exercises, but really anybody can sing it anywhere. It is very good for keeping the feet warm, which is really why Pooh made it up.

March time

The more it SNOWS tiddely-pom,
The more it GOES tiddely-pom
The more it GOES tiddely-pom
On Snowing
On Snowing.

And nobody KNOWS tiddely-pom,
How cold my TOES tiddely-pom
How cold my TOES tiddely-pom
Are Growing,
Are Growing.

Tra-la-la, tra-la-la,
Tra-la-la, tra-la-la.
Rum-tum-tiddle-um-tum.
Tiddle-iddle, tiddle-iddle,
Tiddle-iddle, tiddle-iddle,
Rum-tum-tum-tiddle-um.
    (repeat)

What shall we do about poor little Tigger?

Tigger was a very Bouncy Animal, and when he first came to the Forest, it was a long time before anybody could discover what he liked for breakfast. Pooh made up a song about it. He put in the last two lines because Piglet, who was a Very Small Animal, thought that Tigger bounced too much.

Sadly

What shall we do about poor little Tigger?
If he never eats nothing he'll never get bigger.
He doesn't like honey and haycorns and
thistles
Because of the taste and because of the
bristles.

And all the good things which an animal likes
Have the wrong sort of swallow or too many
spikes.
But whatever his weight in pounds, shillings
and ounces,
He always seems bigger because of his bounces.
Bounces.

I could spend a happy morning . . .

One day Pooh sat in the Sun, and wondered what to do. First of all he thought he would go and see Kanga and Roo . . . and then he thought he would go and see Rabbit (who always said 'Help yourself' and 'What about another slice?') . . . and then he thought that most of all, he would like to see his favourite friend, Piglet. In the three verses of this song you can hear him trying to make up his mind. If the last verse isn't very good, you must remember that it was the sort of lazy, sunny day when nobody really bothers.

Consideringly

I could spend a happy morning
Seeing Roo,
I could spend a happy morning
Being Pooh.
For it doesn't seem to matter,
If I don't get any fatter
(And I *don't* get any fatter),
What I do.

Oh, I like his way of talking,
Yes, I do.
It's the nicest way of talking
Just for two.
And a Help yourself with Rabbit
Tho' it may become a habit,
Is a *pleasant* sort of habit
For a Pooh.

I could spend a happy morning
Seeing Piglet.
And I couldn't spend a happy morning
Not seeing Piglet.
And it doesn't seem to matter
If I don't see Owl or Eeyore
    (or any of the others),
And I'm not going to see Owl or Eeyore
    (or any of the others)
Or Christopher Robin.

Oh, *the Butterflies*
are flying

This song is known as 'Noise, by Pooh.' He 'Sort of made it up' one spring day. As he explained to Rabbit, 'It isn't Brain, because You Know Why, Rabbit; but it comes to me sometimes,' and Rabbit who never let things come to him, but always went and fetched them, said 'Ah!' encouragingly.

Happily

Oh, the butterflies are flying,
Now the winter days are dying,
And the primroses are trying
To be seen.

And the turtle-doves are cooing,
And the woods are up and doing,
For the violets are blueing,
In the green.

Oh, the honey-bees are gumming
On their little wings, and humming
That the summer, which is coming,
Will be fun.

And the cows are almost cooing,
And the turtle-doves are mooing,
Which is why a Pooh is pooh-ing
In the sun.

For the spring is really springing;
You can see the skylark singing,
And the bluebells which are ringing,
Can be heard.

And the cuckoo isn't cooing,
But he's cucking and he's ooing,
And a Pooh is simply pooh-ing
Like a bird.

If Rabbit was bigger . . .

One day Rabbit decided that It Couldn't Go On Any Longer. Tigger was getting too Bouncy and must be unbounced. And when he heard this, Pooh made up a very quiet Hum which he hummed to himself.

Quickly

If Rabbit
Was bigger
And fatter
And stronger,
Or bigger
Than Tigger,

If Tigger was smaller,
Then Tigger's bad habit
Of bouncing at Rabbit
Would matter
No longer,
If Rabbit
Was taller.

If Tigger was smaller,
Then Tigger's bad habit
Of bouncing at Rabbit
Would matter
No longer,
If Rabbit
Was taller.

If Rabbit
Was taller.
But he isn't (*Spoken*)

This Warm and Sunny Spot . . .

This song was made up by Pooh in a Thoughtful Spot where he and Piglet used to meet, but if I say any more about it, the Explanation will be longer than the Song.

Sunnily

This warm and sunny spot
Belongs to Pooh.
And here he wonders what
He's going to do.
Oh, bother, I forgot,
Oh, bother, I forgot,
It's Piglet's too.
Oh, bother, I forgot
It's Piglet's too.

'Sorry, Piglet!' (*Spoken*)

I lay on my Chest . . .

Pooh and Piglet were having tea with Owl one blusterous day, and suddenly Owl's house was blown down, and all the furniture in the sitting-room rushed up to the ceiling and the ceiling rushed down to the floor, and nobody knew where anybody else was. For a long time Pooh was completely missing, and it wasn't until one of the chairs began to talk that Piglet thought of looking in the right place. This is the song which Pooh made up while he was waiting to be rescued.

Breathlessly

I lay on my chest
And I thought it was best
To pretend I was having an evening rest;
I lay on my tum
And I tried to hum
But nothing particular seemed to come.

My face was flat
On the floor, and that
Is all very well for an acrobat;
But it doesn't seem fair
To a Friendly Bear
To stiffen him out with a basket-chair.

And a sort of sqoze
Which grows and grows
Is not too nice for his poor old nose,
And a sort of squch
Is much too much
For his neck and his mouth and his ears and
                                        such.

Here lies a Tree

This is a Respectful Pooh Song in praise of Piglet, and describes so exactly what happened when Owl's house blew down that I shan't say any more about it.

Dramatically

Here lies a tree which Owl (a bird)
Was fond of when it stood on end,
And Owl was talking to a friend
Called Me (in case you hadn't heard)
When something Oo occurred.

More brightly

For lo! the wind was blusterous
And flattened out his fav'rite tree;
And things looked bad for him and we—
Looked bad, I mean, for he and us—
I've never known them wuss.

Then Piglet (PIGLET) thought a thing:
'Courage!' he said. 'There's always hope.
I want a thinnish piece of rope.
Or, if there isn't any, bring
A thickish piece of string.'

With more spirit

So to the letter-box he rose,
While Pooh and Owl said 'Oh!' and 'Hum!'
And where the letters always come
(Called 'LETTERS ONLY') Piglet sqoze
His head and then his toes.

O gallant Piglet (PIGLET)! Ho!
Did Piglet tremble? Did he blinch?
No, no, he struggled inch by inch.
Through LETTERS ONLY, as I know
Because I saw him go.

Excitedly

He ran and ran, and then he stood
And shouted, 'Help for Owl, a bird,
And Pooh, a bear!' until he heard
The others coming through the wood
As quickly as they could.

As when singing Grand Opera [*Next line Ed.*]

'Help-help and Rescue!' Piglet cried,
And showed the others where to go.
[Sing ho! for Piglet (PIGLET) ho!]
And soon the door was opened wide,
And we were both outside!
Sing ho! for Piglet, ho!
Ho!

Christopher Robin is going

This song oughtn't to be in the book really, because it was written by Eeyore, the old grey donkey. 'Hitherto,' as he explained to the other animals, 'all the Poetry in the Forest has been written by Pooh, a bear with a Pleasing Manner but a Positively Startling Lack of Brain,' and when he had read it to them, and Pooh had said admiringly, 'It's much better than mine,' Eeyore explained modestly that it was meant to be. But I don't think it is; and I put it in here, in a book of Pooh Songs partly because it shows that Poetry and Hums are more difficult than people suppose, and partly because it says good-bye to Pooh's great friend, Christopher Robin.

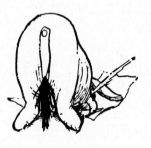

eOR

Wistfully

Christopher Robin is going.
At least I think he is.
Where?
Nobody knows.
But he is going—
I mean he goes
(*To rhyme with 'knows'*)
Do we care?
(*To rhyme with 'where'*)
We do very much.
(*I haven't got a rhyme for that 'is' in the second
   line yet. Bother.*)
(*Now I haven't got a rhyme for that bother.
   Bother.*)

Those two bothers will have to rhyme with
each other.
Buther.
The fact is this is more difficult than I thought
I ought—
(*Very good indeed*)
I ought
To begin again,
But it's easier to stop.

Christopher Robin, good-bye,
I
(Good)
I
And all your friends
Sends

I mean all your friend
Send—
(Very awkward this, it keeps going wrong)
Well, anyhow, we send
Our love—we send
Our love—we send
Our love—
Well, anyhow, we send,
Our love
END.

Pooh